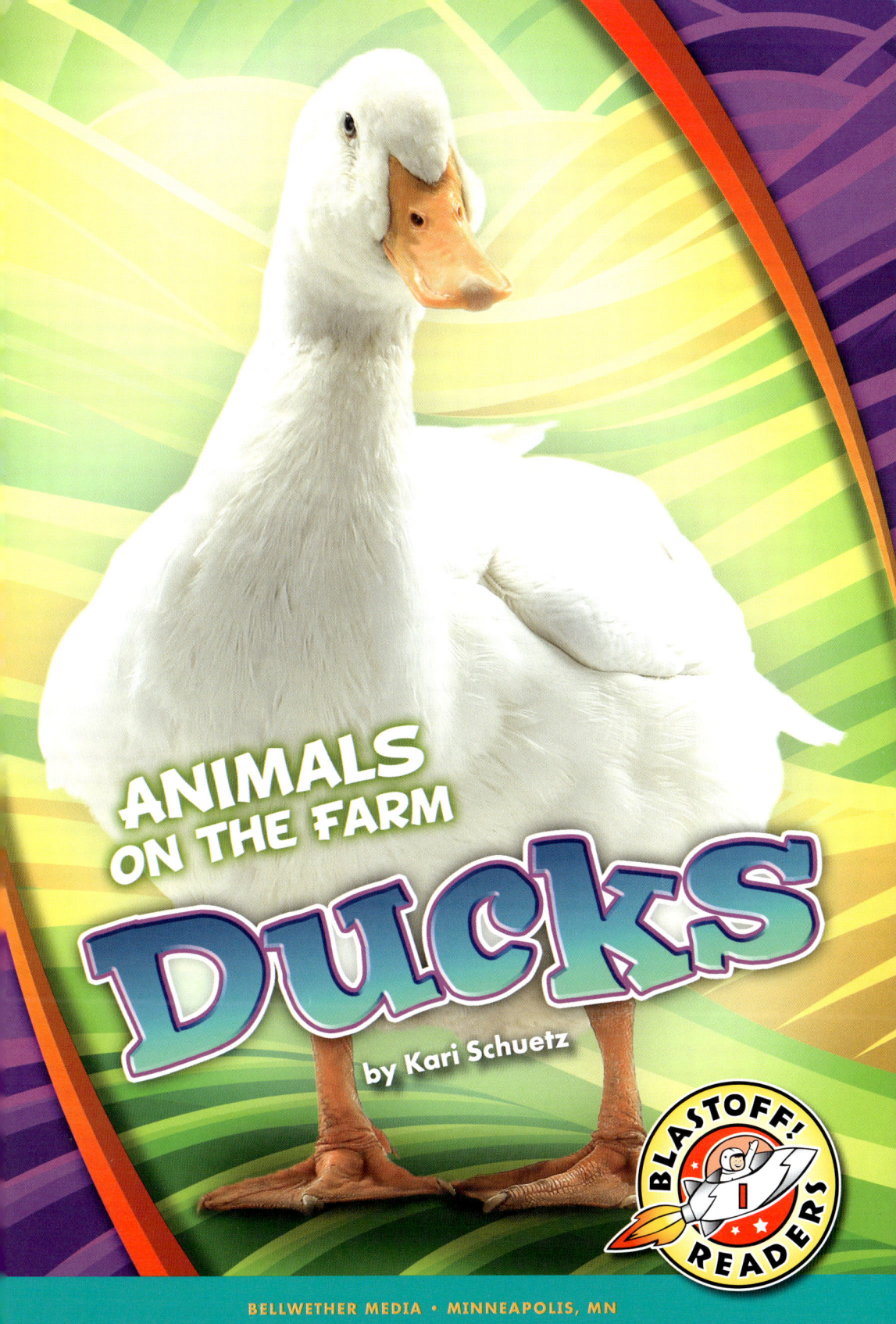

ANIMALS ON THE FARM

Ducks

by Kari Schuetz

BELLWETHER MEDIA • MINNEAPOLIS, MN

Note to Librarians, Teachers, and Parents:

Blastoff! Readers are carefully developed by literacy experts and combine standards-based content with developmentally appropriate text.

Level 1 provides the most support through repetition of high-frequency words, light text, predictable sentence patterns, and strong visual support.

Level 2 offers early readers a bit more challenge through varied simple sentences, increased text load, and less repetition of high-frequency words.

Level 3 advances early-fluent readers toward fluency through increased text and concept load, less reliance on visuals, longer sentences, and more literary language.

Level 4 builds reading stamina by providing more text per page, increased use of punctuation, greater variation in sentence patterns, and increasingly challenging vocabulary.

Level 5 encourages children to move from "learning to read" to "reading to learn" by providing even more text, varied writing styles, and less familiar topics.

Whichever book is right for your reader, Blastoff! Readers are the perfect books to build confidence and encourage a love of reading that will last a lifetime!

This edition first published in 2018 by Bellwether Media, Inc.

No part of this publication may be reproduced in whole or in part without written permission of the publisher. For information regarding permission, write to Bellwether Media, Inc., Attention: Permissions Department, 5357 Penn Avenue South, Minneapolis, MN 55419.

Library of Congress Cataloging-in-Publication Data

Names: Schuetz, Kari, author.
Title: Ducks / by Kari Schuetz.
Description: Minneapolis, MN : Bellwether Media, Inc., [2018] | Series: Blastoff! Readers. Animals on the Farm | Audience: Age 5-8. | Audience: K to Grade 3. | Includes bibliographical references and index.
Identifiers: LCCN 2017029536 | ISBN 9781626177222 (hardcover : alk. paper) | ISBN 9781681035024 (ebook)
Subjects: LCSH: Ducks–Juvenile literature. | CYAC: Ducks.
Classification: LCC SF505.3 .S386 2018 | DDC 636.5/97–dc23
LC record available at https://lccn.loc.gov/2017029536

Editor: Rebecca Sabelko   Designer: Lois Stanfield

Printed in the United States of America, North Mankato, MN.

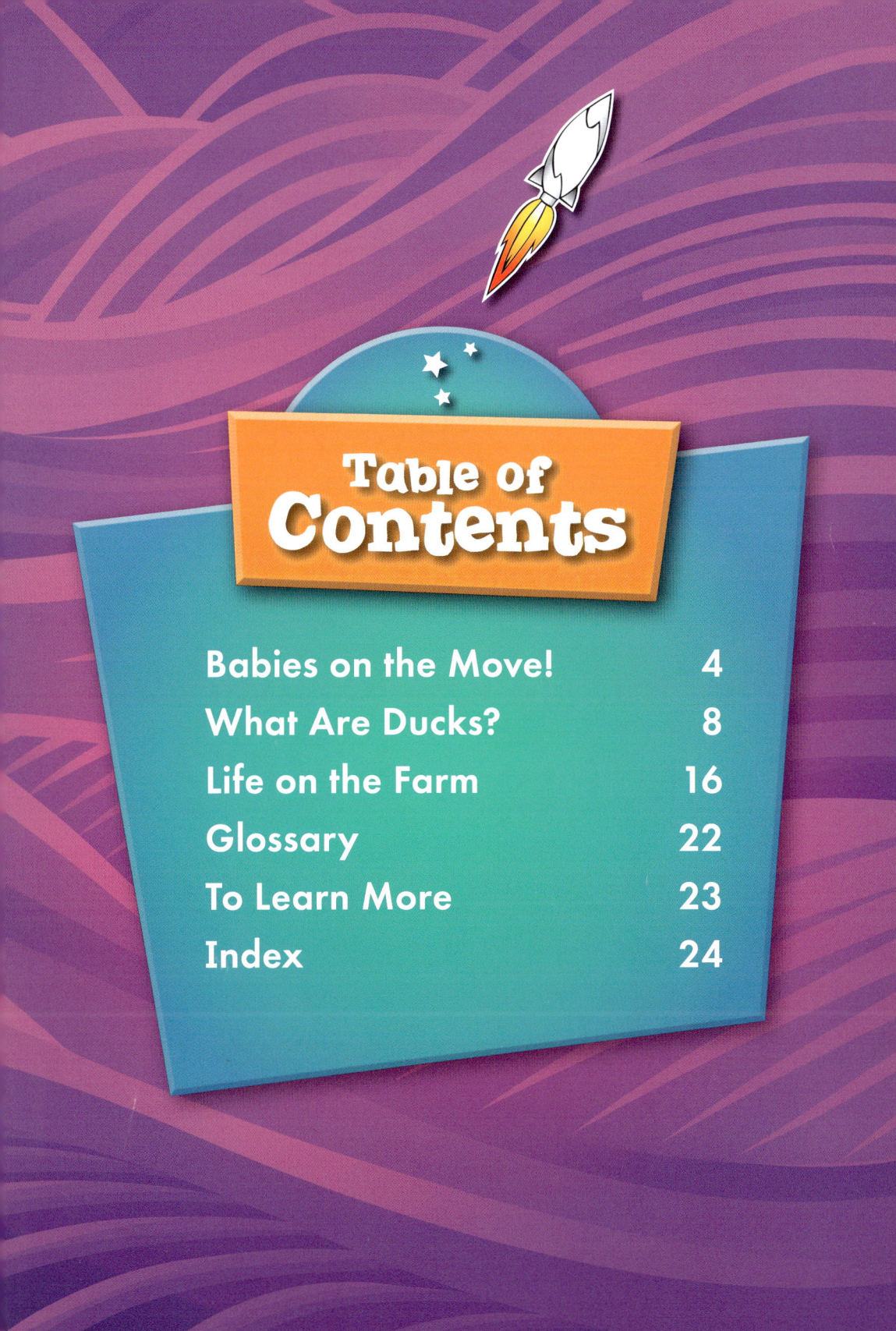

Table of Contents

Babies on the Move!

A farmer watches little ducklings leave their nest. They form a line behind their mom.

ducklings

The ducklings
make their way
to the pond.
Time for a swim!

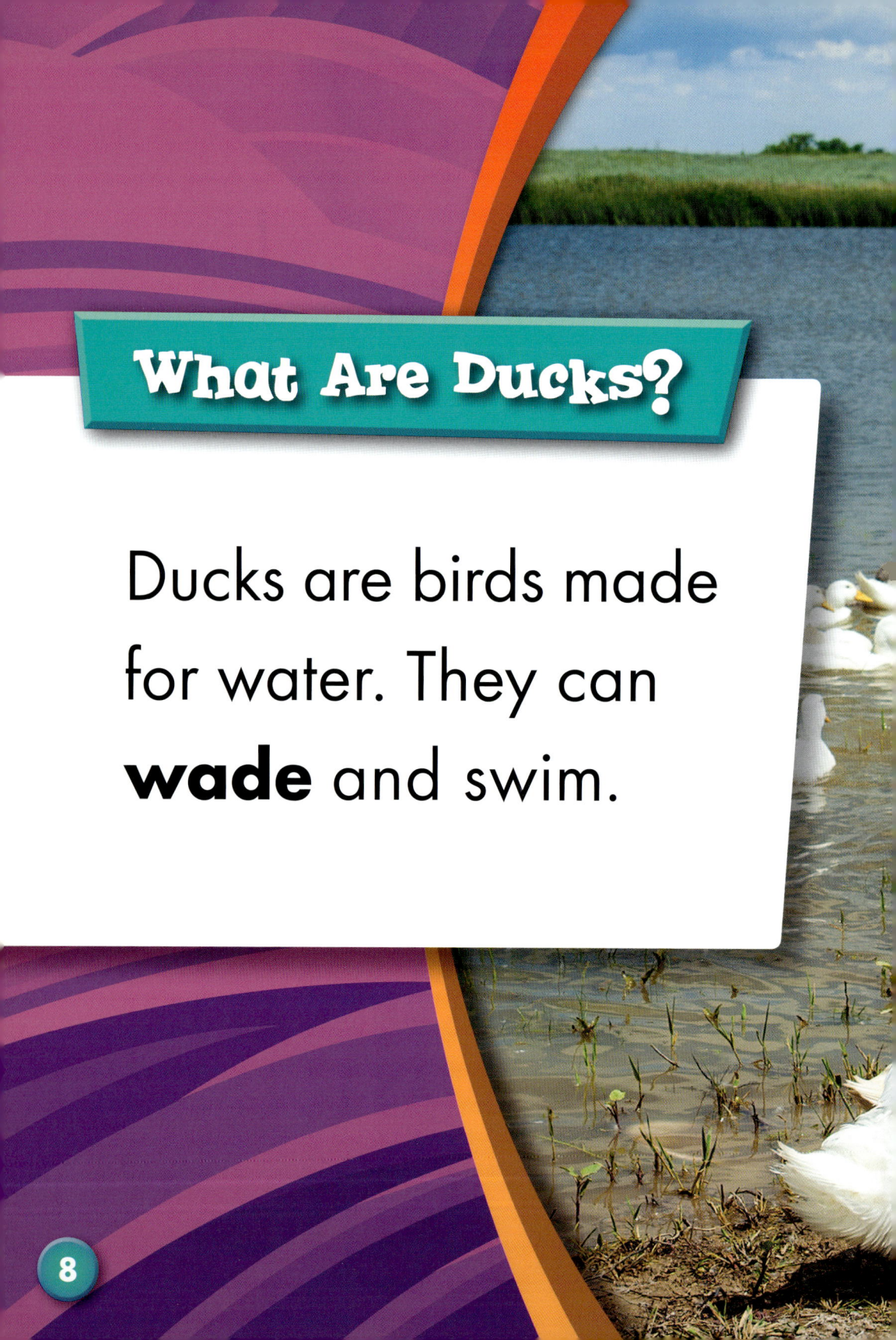

What Are Ducks?

Ducks are birds made for water. They can **wade** and swim.

NAMES:

males:	drakes
females:	ducks
babies:	ducklings

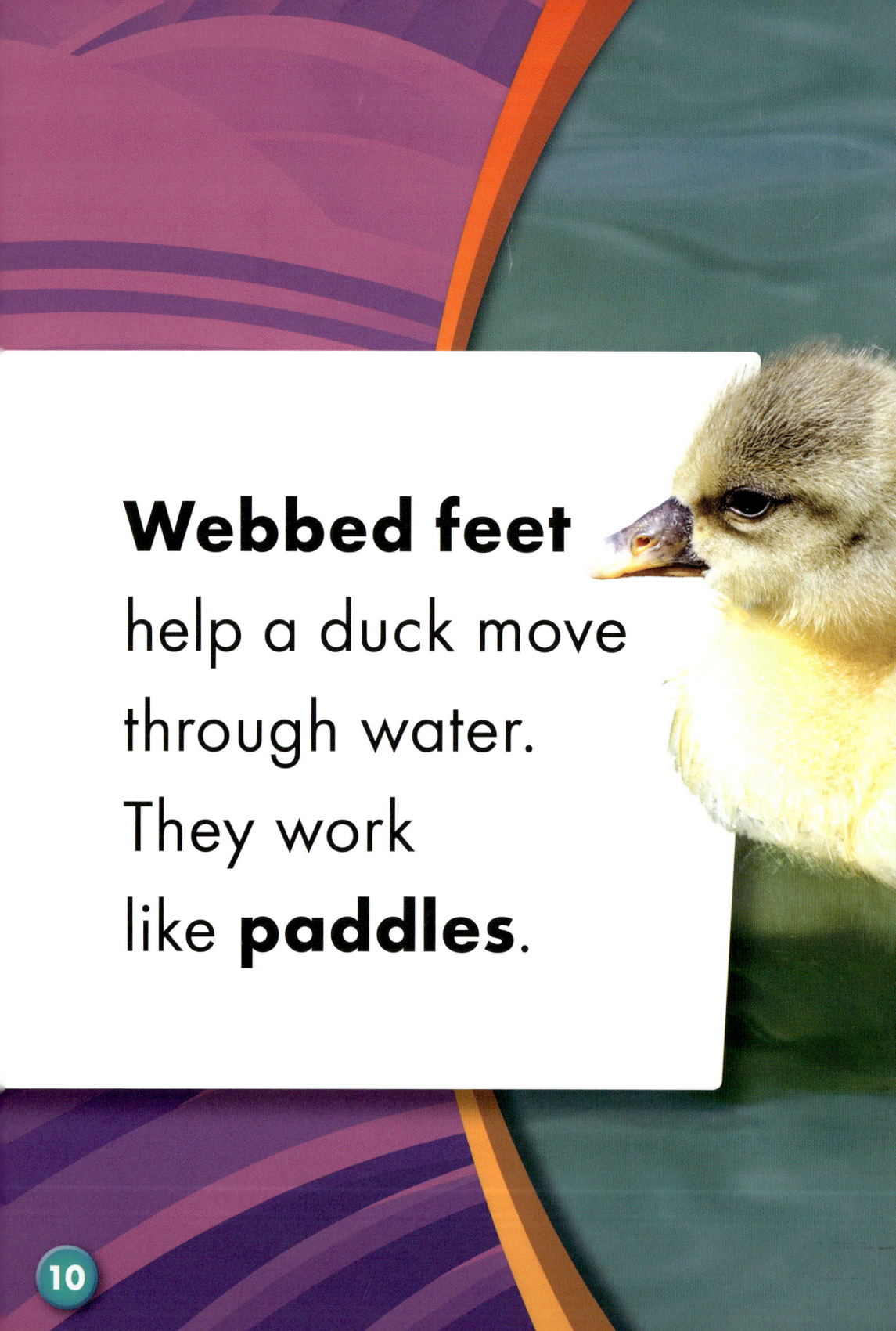

Webbed feet help a duck move through water. They work like **paddles**.

webbed feet

Waterproof

feathers keep the duck dry.

The feathers have a special **oily** coating. This oil is spread with the duck's flat bill.

bill

Life on the Farm

Ducks stay near puddles and ponds. They dip headfirst into the water.

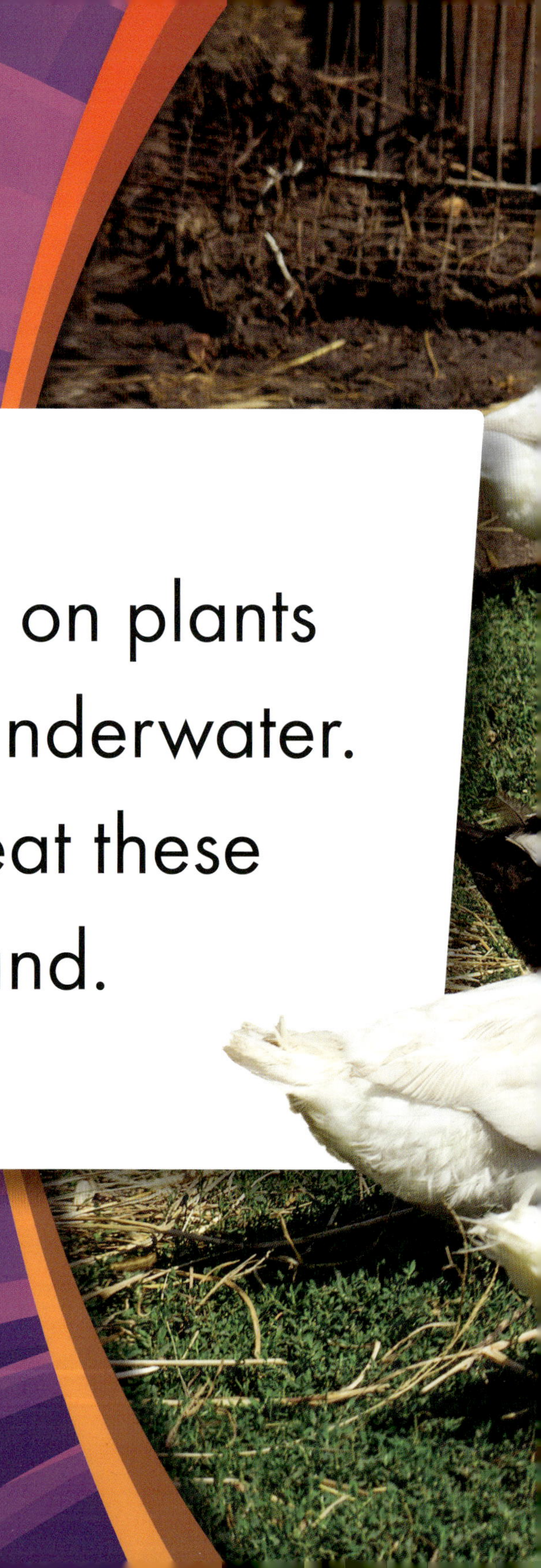

They snack on plants and bugs underwater. They also eat these foods on land.

FAVORITE FOODS:
feed, plants, bugs

19

Ducks quack and flap their wings for **feed**. Farmer, we're hungry!

Glossary

feed

farm food made up of a mixture of grains

wade

to walk in water

oily

coated with a slippery liquid

waterproof

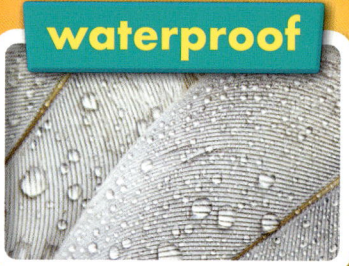

able to stay dry in wet areas

paddles

poles with flat blades; people use paddles to move boats in water.

webbed feet

feet with toes connected by thin skin

To Learn More

AT THE LIBRARY

Delano, Marfé Ferguson. *Ducklings*. Washington, D.C.: National Geographic Kids, 2017.

Gibbs, Maddie. *Ducks*. New York, N.Y.: PowerKids Press, 2015.

Leaf, Christina. *Baby Ducks*. Minneapolis, Minn.: Bellwether Media, 2014.

ON THE WEB

Learning more about ducks is as easy as 1, 2, 3.

1. Go to www.factsurfer.com.

2. Enter "ducks" into the search box.

3. Click the "Surf" button and you will see a list of related web sites.

With factsurfer.com, finding more information is just a click away.

Index